GRANDMA'S
BASEBALL

GAVIN CURTIS

Crown Publishers, Inc.
New York

Published by Crown Publishers, Inc., a Random House Company, 225 Park
Avenue South, New York, New York 10003.
CROWN is a trademark of Crown Publishers, Inc.

Manufactured in the United States.

Library of Congress Cataloging-in-Publication Data
Curtis, Gavin. Grandma's baseball / Gavin Curtis. Summary: A young boy
learns to see beyond his grandmother's grumpiness when she comes to live
with his family following her husband's death.
ISBN 0-517-57389-X   ISBN 0-517-57390-3 (lib. bdg.) [1. Grandmothers–
Fiction.] I. Title PZ7.C9415Gr 1990 [E]–dc20 89-22227

10 9 8 7 6 5 4 3 2 1

First Edition

To Nanny and Mom

One night at dinner Mom and Dad
made an announcement.

"Grandma is coming to live
with us," they said.

My grandmother lives far away. I've only seen her twice in my life. One time was when I was little and the other was last year at Grandpa's funeral.

When Grandpa was young, he played baseball for a team called the Monarchs. When they buried him, they placed his old uniform on top of his casket. Mom cried but Grandma didn't. She just looked sort of grumpy.

I went with Mom and Dad to meet
Grandma's plane. At the airport a
voice over the loudspeaker said that
Grandma's flight had just landed. A few
minutes later we saw Grandma with
two big suitcases.

Driving home, I sat in the backseat. Grandma sat next to me. I showed her where I go to school. She told me to take my foot off the seat.

Mom and Dad asked me to take
the smaller guest room. Grandma
moved her things into my room.

The next morning Grandma made breakfast—oatmeal. I hate oatmeal. Grandma says it's full of vitamins and stuff. She says she will be fixing breakfast from now on. I hate breakfast.

Later, Mom, Grandma, and I took
a walk through the park.

"Let's get a cherry ice pop," I said.

Grandma said, "No, it's too close to
suppertime."

Grandma told me not to slam the
screen door when I went out to play...

...and when I came back in.

I didn't like when Grandma came
to walk me home from school. We never
stopped to feed the ducks in the pond,
the way Mom and I did.

"You have homework to do,"
Grandma would say.

One morning, after breakfast, I walked past Grandma's bedroom and noticed an old baseball on top of her dresser. It was a little yellow and had writing all over it. Maybe it used to belong to Grandpa?

I took the ball out to the backyard
to see if it still worked.

I tried knocking a can off the porch, but I missed. The ball hit the screen door with a thud. "Are you still slamming that...?" Grandma started to say, but stopped when she noticed the ball.

I thought she was going to be mad.
Instead, Grandma picked up Grandpa's
baseball and brushed it off.

"You're doing it all wrong," she said, and showed me a different way to hold the ball. I tried it again. This time I hit the can with one pitch.

"That one is called a sinker," Grandma said.

"Wow," I said. "Where did you learn that?"

But she didn't answer. Grandma didn't look grumpy anymore. She looked sort of sad.

Soon she said, "Your grandfather taught me that pitch when your mother was smaller than you."

Then Grandma started to cry.

I hugged Grandma and told her
not to be sad. I think that made her feel
a little better. "I love you," she said.

"I love you, too, Grandma." Then I
said, "Do you think you could lighten
up on the oatmeal?"

"Sure," she answered, "if you
promise to lighten up on the screen
door."